¡Hola! I'm Dora and this is my friend Boots. We're goin[...] star-catching adventure to Star Mountain. Will you be [...] Catcher with us? We'll need the special decoder inside [...] book. We can use it to see the hidden answers that the arrow is pointing to.

And don't forget to watch for Swiper the fox. If you see him, say, "Swiper, no swiping!"

The Map says we need to go through the Dark Forest and then over Turtle Stream. That's how we'll get to Star Mountain.

Look, stars! ¡Estrellas! Boots and I each caught 2 stars. Help us add my 2 stars to his 2 stars by counting all the stars we have together. Write the number and use the decoder to check your answer.

2 + 2 = _____

Smart adding! Let's put the stars in my star pocket.

It's too dark in the Dark Forest to see any stars. Boots didn't catch any stars, and neither did I. Did we catch any stars at all?

$$0 + 0 = \underline{}$$

No, we didn't. We need an Explorer Star to help us see in the dark. Do you know which Explorer Star can help us?

It's Glowy, the bright light Explorer Star! Glowy is shining so we can see the stars! Thanks, Glowy.

Boots and I each caught 1 purple star. Add them together.

1 + 1 = _____

And look! More stars to catch in the Dark Forest! How many blue stars are there? Count them and write the number.

Let's add Glowy to the 4 blue stars we just caught in the Dark Forest.

4 + 1 = _____

Add each pair of numbers and write the total. Then draw a line to the star that shows the total.

3 + 2 = _____

3 + 4 = _____

2 + 1 = _____

4 + 2 = _____

6 + 4 = _____

3

5

7

10

6

I just caught 2 more stars and Boots caught 1. How many do we have together?

2 + 1 = _____

Oh, no. There are branches blocking the path! We need an Explorer Star to help us. Which Explorer Star can blow the branches out of our way?

It's Gusty, the windy Explorer Star! Gusty blew the branches out of our way. Thanks, Gusty!

Look, there are more stars! ¡Más estrellas! How many green stars do you see? Circle them and write the number.

Help us add Gusty to the 3 green stars we just caught.

$$3 + 1 = \text{\_\_\_\_}$$

We just caught more stars! Boots caught 3 and I caught 2. How many did we catch together?

3 + 2 = _____

Add each pair of numbers and write the total. Then draw a line to the star that shows the total.

9 + 1 = _____

1 + 6 = _____

5 + 3 = _____

2 + 7 = _____

3 + 1 = _____

7

4

10

8

9

13

We made it to Turtle Stream! Boots caught 2 more stars on this side of the stream, but I didn't catch any. How many is that?

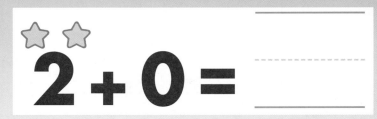

2 + 0 = _____

We need an Explorer Star to help us cross the water. Which Explorer Star can help us?

It's Saltador, the super jumping Explorer Star! Saltador helped us jump over Turtle Stream. Thanks, Saltador!

And look! There are pink stars on this side! How many pink stars do you see? Catch them, catch them! Circle them and write the number.

Now, let's add Saltador to the 5 pink stars we just caught.

5
+1
___

I just caught 1 more star, but Boots didn't catch any. How many stars did we just catch all together?

$$\begin{array}{r} 1\ \bigstar \\ +\ 0 \\ \hline \end{array}$$

Adding down is the same as adding across! Add these numbers then circle in the correct answer below each problem.

7
+2

7   8   (9)

6
+2

7   8   9

4
+5

7   8   9

1
+5

4   5   6

3
+3

4   5   6

We're almost to the top of Star Mountain. Look! More stars! Boots caught 4 stars and so did I. How many is that all together? Write the number and check your answer.

$$4$$
$$+4$$
_____

Uh, oh. I see Swiper. That sneaky fox will try to swipe the stars we caught! Say, "Swiper, no swiping!"

Thanks for helping us stop Swiper!

We made it to the top of Star Mountain! There are lots of stars to catch here. I caught 5 and so did Boots. Let's add them together.

5 + 5 = _____

We caught so many stars today! Count and color all the stars we caught. How many did you count? Use your decoder to check your answer.

Thanks for helping! You're a great Star Catcher!

What kind of Explorer Star would you like to meet? Connect the dots from 1 to 10 and color the picture to finish your Explorer Star.

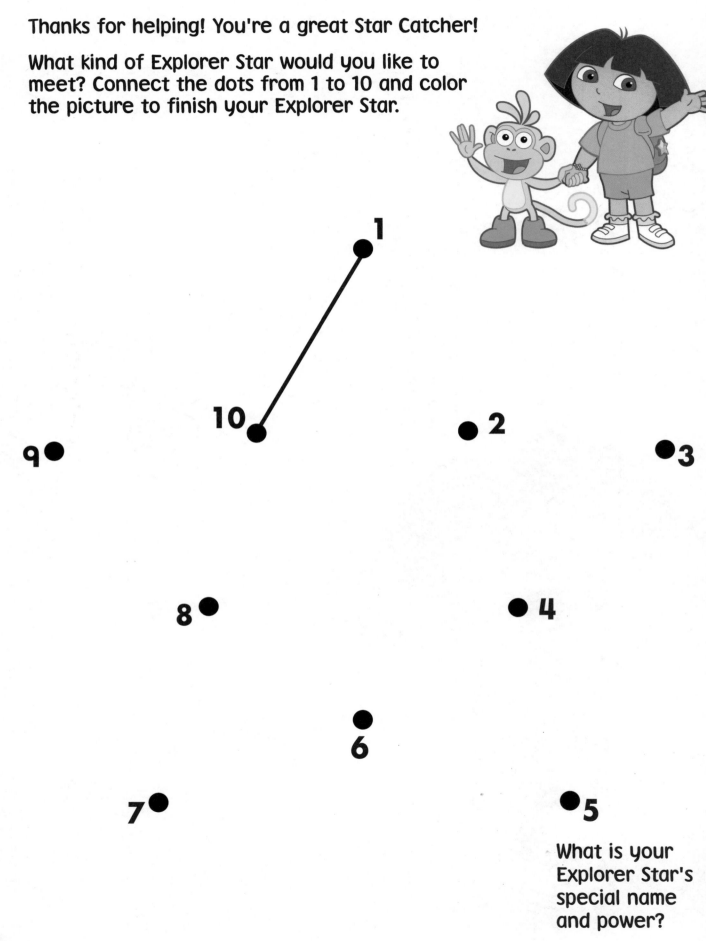

1

10

2

9

3

8

4

6

7

5

What is your Explorer Star's special name and power?